With our love &
wishing you God's blessings,
Great Uncle Fred & Aunt Julie

(note that our daughter, Kimberly,
did the illustrations in this book)

RABBITS ON MARS

BY JAN WAHL

PICTURES BY
KIMBERLY SCHAMBER

CAROLRHODA BOOKS, INC. · MINNEAPOLIS

Feeling hungry, Greenleaf looked about. "It's not easy
to be a rabbit," he sighed. "Where do new carrots grow?"

Ouzel shook long ears, agreeing. "I hear nowadays they
grow in things called greenhouses."

"Maybe we'll find carrots on the other side of the
highway," added tiny Peppercorn.

So they waited for traffic to pass. "You take life in your paws," said Greenleaf, "just to cross the road!" The three raced to the other side, just in the nick of time, before a long truck rumbled by.

In the middle of the night in a field, with flashlight and spade, the rabbits dug. No carrots!

Then it began to rain. They found a summer cabin that sat empty, nearby. In a cupboard lay crackers and biscuits and a tin of soup. Working together, they opened the can.

"Oh—it's only noodle soup," said Ouzel.

"I wish it was carrot soup," said Peppercorn.

After the soup, they felt like dancing. There was a radio so they switched it on and danced until sunup. Ouzel and Greenleaf did a wild jitterbug. Peppercorn danced upside down.

Going home through a small woods,
they were chased by a loud, spotted dog.
The rabbits ran like the wind.
   "We're only a flash of fur!" said
Greenleaf.

"Why can't we ever
meet friendly dogs?"
Ouzel wondered.
"I wish we lived someplace
without them!" said Peppercorn.
Luckily the three reached home,
which was a safe hole. They dived
in and slept the whole day
snuggled together.

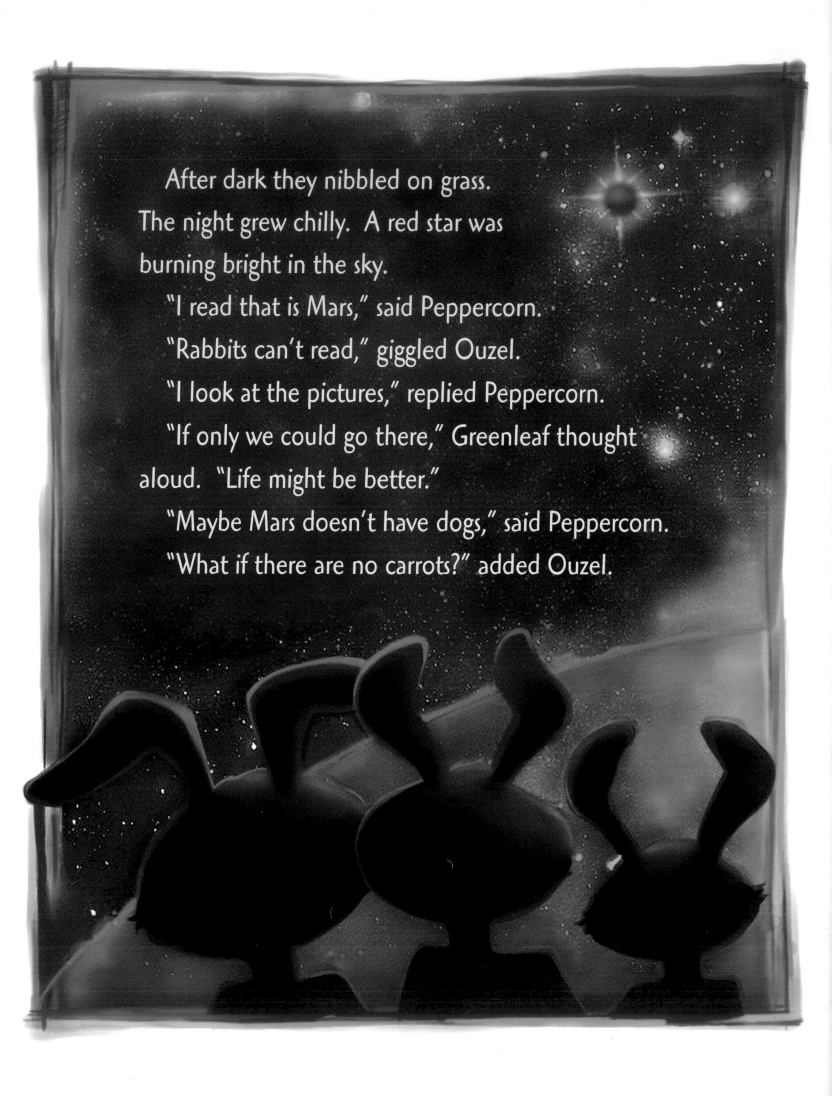

After dark they nibbled on grass.
The night grew chilly. A red star was
burning bright in the sky.

"I read that is Mars," said Peppercorn.

"Rabbits can't read," giggled Ouzel.

"I look at the pictures," replied Peppercorn.

"If only we could go there," Greenleaf thought
aloud. "Life might be better."

"Maybe Mars doesn't have dogs," said Peppercorn.

"What if there are no carrots?" added Ouzel.

Suddenly a strong wind blew through their fur. "Winter's coming soon," said Greenleaf. "Our coats are never thick enough!"

He lay thinking hard. Life just *had* to be better on Mars, he decided.

"WE'LL GO TO MARS!" he shouted.

Furry paws kept busy after that. The rabbits collected odds and ends. At an abandoned farm, behind an empty silo, they built a rocket ship. They used pictures from books they found.

Ouzel was good at seeing to details. Peppercorn was tiny but clever at sewing and made impressive space suits.

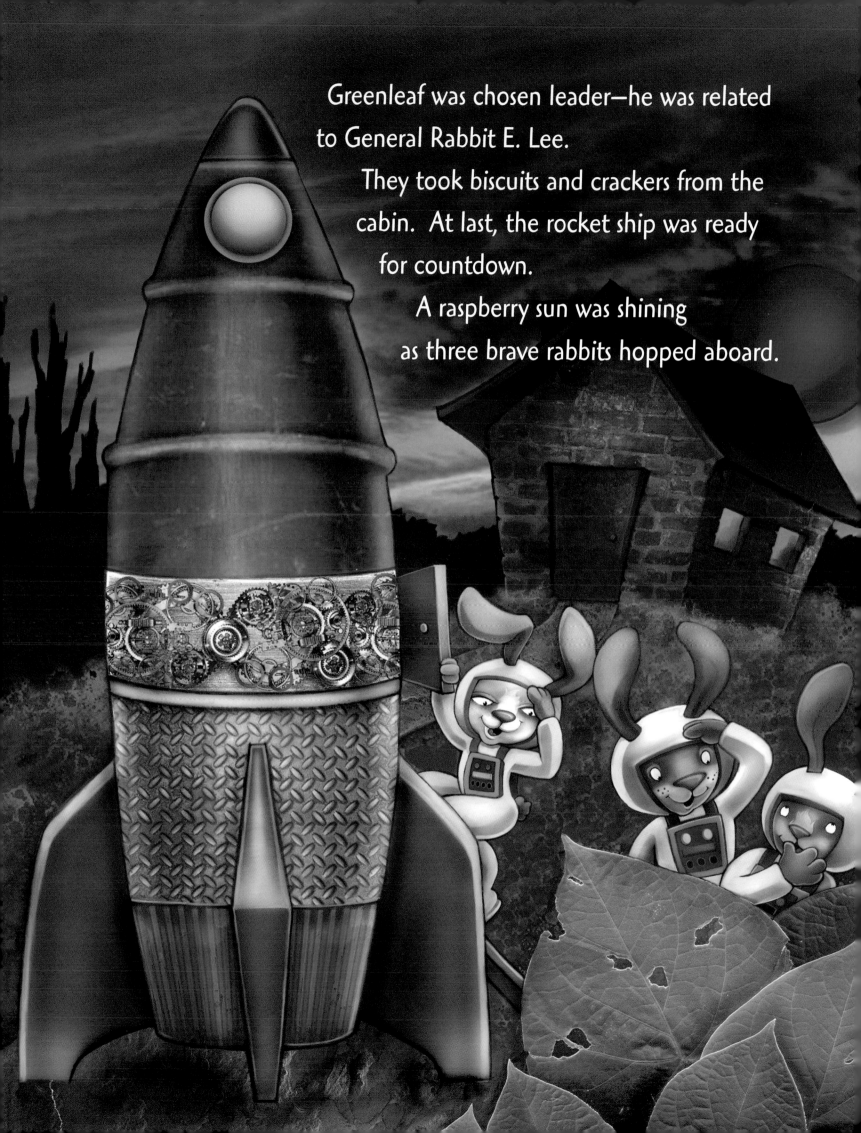

Greenleaf was chosen leader—he was related
to General Rabbit E. Lee.
They took biscuits and crackers from the
cabin. At last, the rocket ship was ready
for countdown.
A raspberry sun was shining
as three brave rabbits hopped aboard.

Takeoff was quick. The whole rocket sputtered and shook. Ka-bing! KA-BING! WUP, WUP, WUP! WWSSSSSHHHH! Heading right for the clouds and beyond.

After they zoomed up far enough, the rabbits removed plugs from their ears. They floated about, hitting noses on the ceiling. When they got hungry each day, they shared a cracker. Or biscuit. Carefully Captain Greenleaf steered them past whizzing meteors.

The crew sang songs to stay calm.
Days grew into weeks, weeks into months.
When they napped, they shared
carrot dreams. Water
was so scarce they
took sponge baths.

Earth grew smaller...
and smaller...and smaller.

Mars grew bigger... and bigger... and bigger.

Until Mars at last lay ahead—very red—with two moons that looked like twin potatoes. **"I don't know how to land this thing,"** cried the captain.

"Let me try," said Peppercorn.

Then he did. BOMP.

"Hooray!" Ouzel shouted.

They opened the rocket ship door and jumped out to stretch their legs on red gravel. Leapfrogging over and over, the rabbits entered a valley. They couldn't believe it!

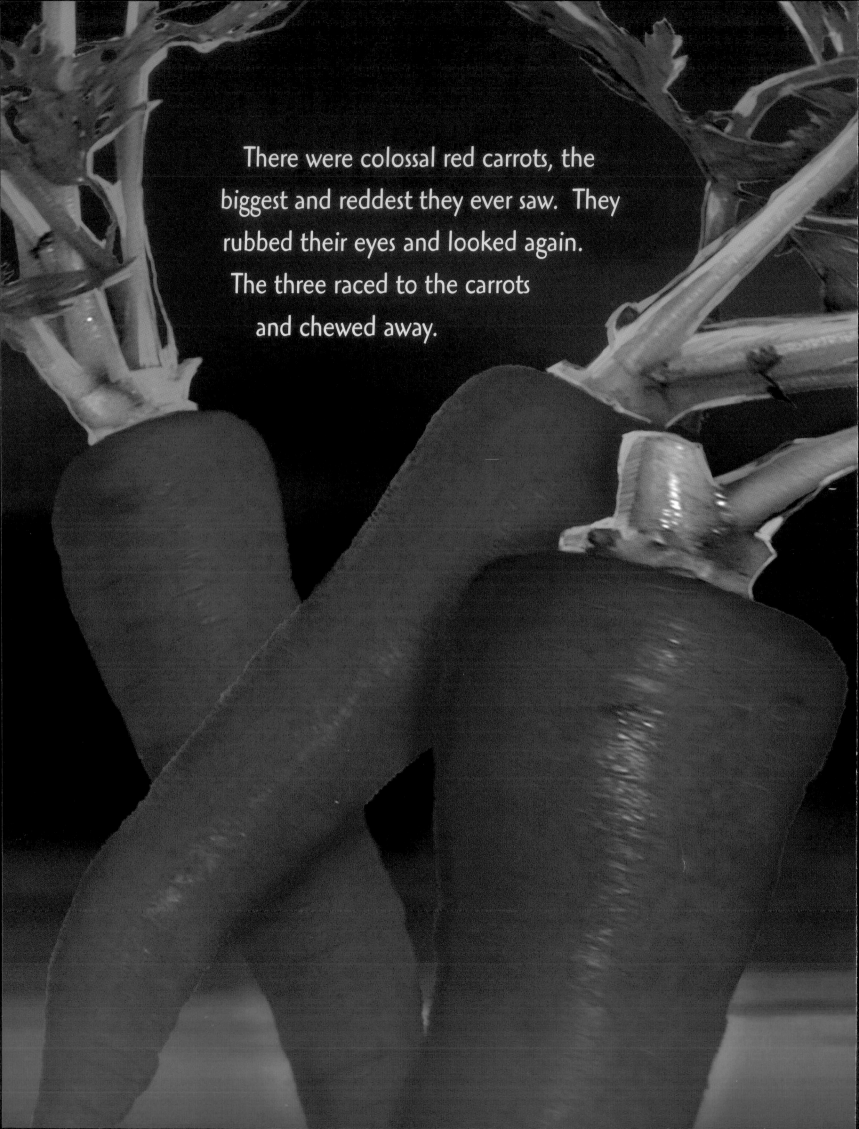

There were colossal red carrots, the
biggest and reddest they ever saw. They
rubbed their eyes and looked again.
The three raced to the carrots
and chewed away.

"Delicious," said Greenleaf.

"Perfect," said Ouzel.

"Big," said Peppercorn.

They ate to their hearts' content. Yum. Burp. Yum. They ate until their tummies hurt.

Greenleaf had to lie down. "Have you noticed," he asked, "how warm it is? Makes me sleepy."

"Whew, me too," gasped Ouzel.

"Too bad we can't take off our coats," said Peppercorn. Finally the three fell asleep.

Ouzel was the first to wake, shouting, "I'm having a nightmare!"

"So am I! And in daylight, too," said Peppercorn.

"Is it happening?" Greenleaf wondered.

A bunch of gigantic green dogs leaned over them.

"SNAPPO! WURDLU!" barked the dogs.

"Uh-oh," groaned Ouzel. "We're done for!"

"S N A P P O! W U R D L U!" the dogs shouted,
wagging giant tails.

"Look at those eyes," said Peppercorn.
"Sort of friendly, I hope."

"Or maybe lonely?" said Ouzel. "They
might just want to play."

"Let's give it a try," said Greenleaf.

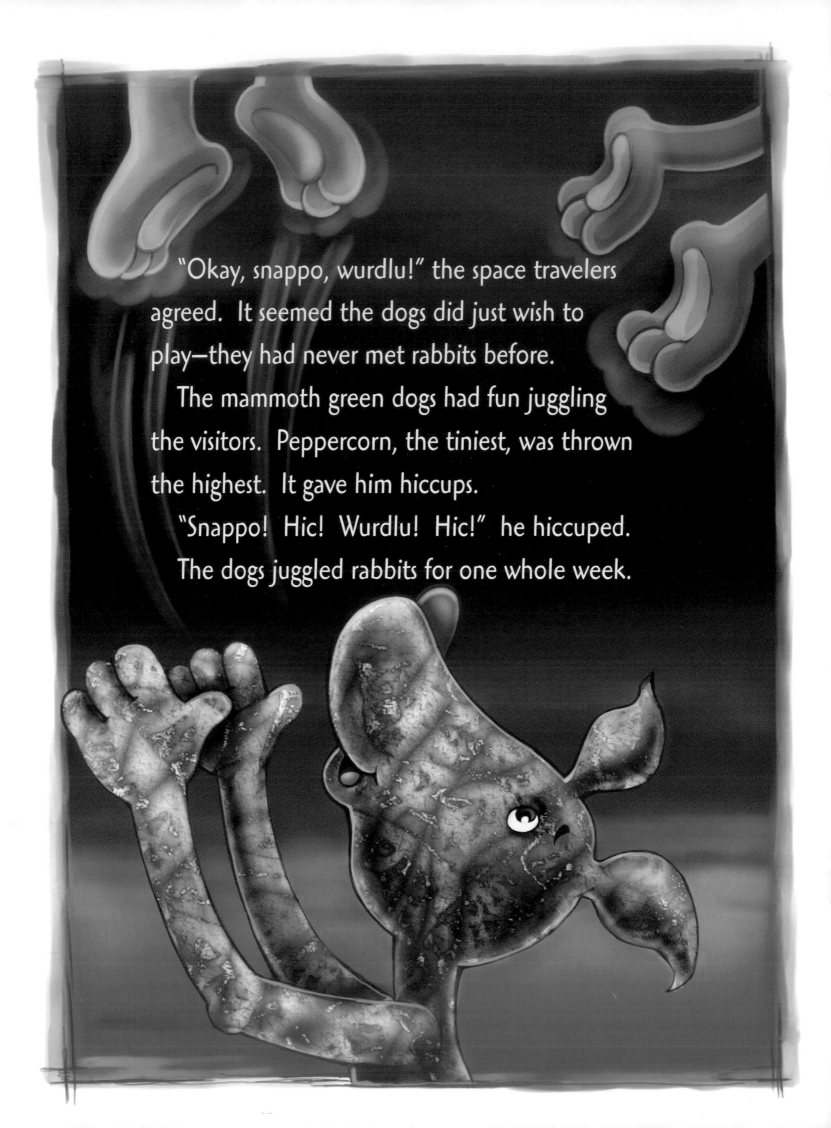

"Okay, snappo, wurdlu!" the space travelers agreed. It seemed the dogs did just wish to play—they had never met rabbits before.

The mammoth green dogs had fun juggling the visitors. Peppercorn, the tiniest, was thrown the highest. It gave him hiccups.

"Snappo! Hic! Wurdlu! Hic!" he hiccuped. The dogs juggled rabbits for one whole week.

Then the dogs wanted to play tennis. Of course,
Peppercorn, being the smallest, was their favorite tennis ball.
The dogs didn't keep score but enjoyed batting their
visitors back and forth.

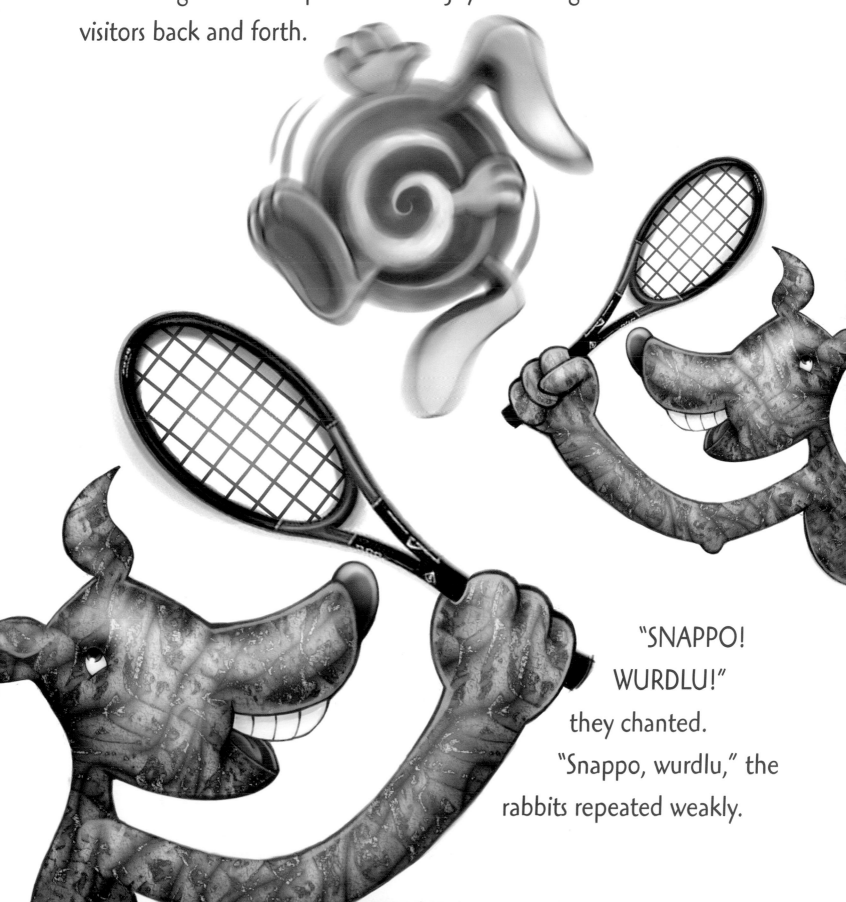

"SNAPPO!
WURDLU!"
they chanted.
"Snappo, wurdlu," the
rabbits repeated weakly.

Next, the dogs wanted to bowl—using Peppercorn as a bowling ball and Ouzel and Greenleaf as bowling pins.

"SNAPPO! WURDLU!"

"Yes, snappo, wurdlu!" the rabbits said.

"It's too hot for this," whispered Ouzel.
"They're too friendly!" groaned Greenleaf.
"I'm sick of carrots," Peppercorn squeaked.

"What can we do?" asked Ouzel.
"I have a plan," said Peppercorn. "Let's teach
them how to jitterbug."

So he whistled as many tunes as he could
remember, and Ouzel and Greenleaf showed them
the jitterbug. Soon, the green dogs were dancing
their heads off at top speed.

They flipped and flopped and whistled along. They
danced among themselves and paid no attention to
their visitors.

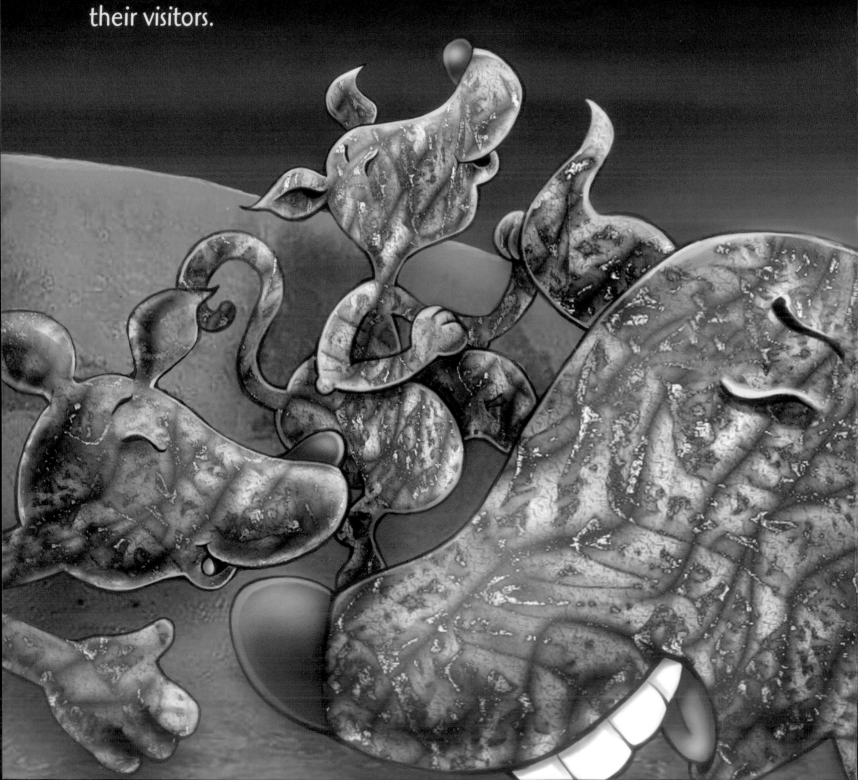

"Let's get out of here," whispered
Peppercorn.
"You're a genius!" Captain
Greenleaf cried out, and the
rabbits rushed off to the
rocket ship.

Since there are no trucks on Mars, they were able to dash out of the valley, across the gravel, and back to the ship without glancing right or left. The dogs didn't notice.

The captain pushed on the throttle.

The rocket ship sputtered and shook. CHUG-GA! CHUG-GA! CHUG-GA! Ka-bing! Ka-bing! WUP, WUP, WUP! WWSSSSSHHHH!

The rabbit vessel shot up
from planet Mars into outer space!
Mars grew smaller . . .

and smaller . . .

and smaller.

Earth grew bigger . . .

and bigger . . .

and bigger.

The first million miles or so were
easy. "Drat!" Captain Greenleaf
suddenly yelled above the din.

"We're out of fuel!"

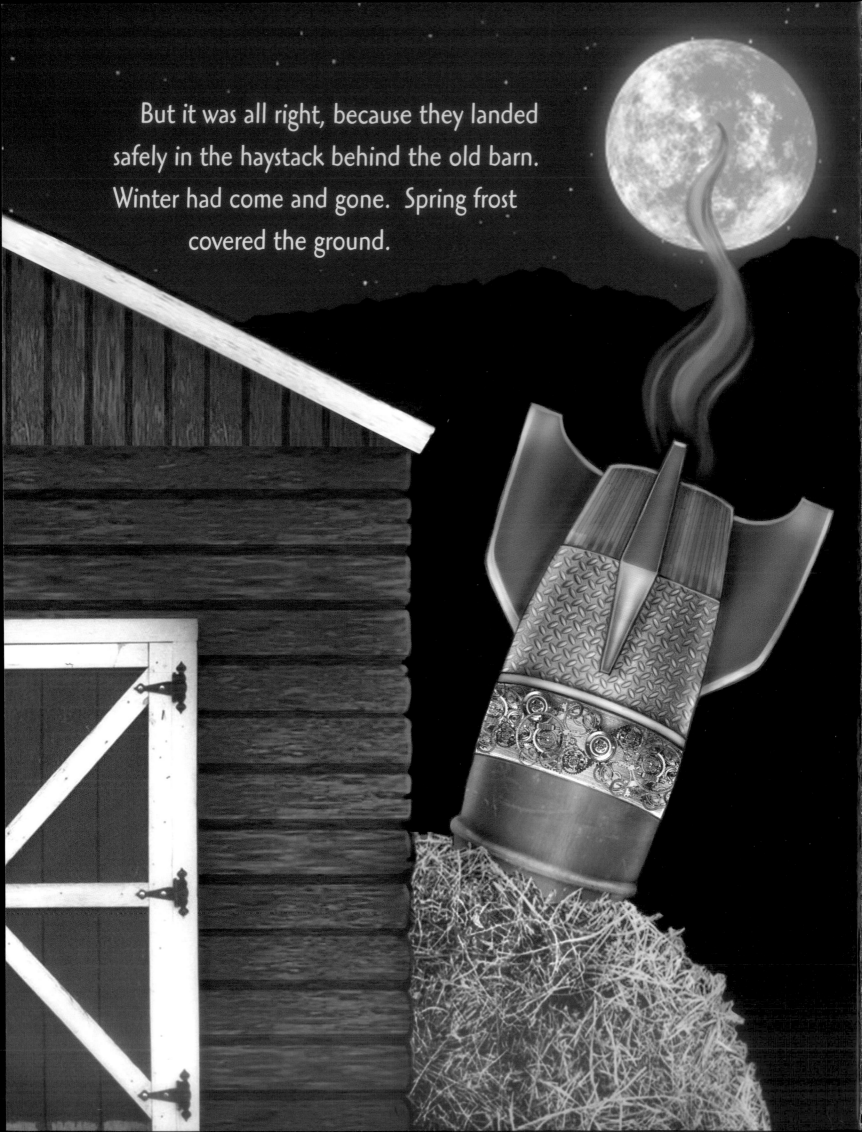

But it was all right, because they landed
safely in the haystack behind the old barn.
Winter had come and gone. Spring frost
covered the ground.

They found some nice tulip bulbs and
leaped back in the haystack where it was snug
and cozy. They happily chewed on the bulbs.

"It's good to be home!" sighed tiny Peppercorn.
"Yes, on Earth we can hide from dogs if we must,"
said Greenleaf.
"And jitterbug the whole night if we wish,"
added Ouzel.

Lying on his back, Peppercorn looked up into the
sky and saw a cool blue star shining so brightly.

"I read that's Jupiter," said Peppercorn.
"I wonder what it's like there . . . "
But Ouzel and Greenleaf were fast asleep.

TO AUSTIN AND EVAN TAYLOR—J.W.

TO SOPHIA AND GRACE LUEHMANN—K.S.

Carolrhoda Books, Inc.
A division of Lerner Publishing Group
241 First Avenue North
Minneapolis, MN 55401 U.S.A.

Website address: www.lernerbooks.com

Library of Congress Cataloging-in-Publication Data

Wahl, Jan.
    Rabbits on Mars / by Jan Wahl ; pictures by Kimberly Schamber.
      p.   cm.
    Summary: Tired of their hard life on Earth, where dogs chase them,
  winters are cold, and carrots scarce, three rabbit friends build a rocket
  ship and journey to Mars in hopes of finding a better life.
    ISBN: 1–57505–511–2 (lib. bdg. : alk. paper)
    [1. Rabbits—Fiction. 2. Space flight to Mars—Fiction.
  3. Contentment—Fiction.] I. Schamber, Kimberly, ill. II. Title.
  PZ7.W1266 Rad 2003
  [Fic]—dc21   2002006780

Manufactured in the United States of America
1 2 3 4 5 6 – JR – 08 07 06 05 04 03